Family Scrapbook

Family Scrapbook

M. B. Goffstein

FARRAR · STRAUS · GIROUX

NEW YORK

Copyright © 1978 by M. B. Goffstein
All rights reserved
Library of Congress catalog card number: 78–51435
Published simultaneously in Canada
by McGraw-Hill Ryerson Ltd., Toronto
Printed in the United States of America
by Halliday Lithograph
Bound by A. Horowitz and Son
Designed by Cynthia Krupat
First edition, 1978

To Michael di Capua

The Night We Got a Pickup Truck

An unfamiliar horn kept beeping,
but I was standing on a busy corner
looking for my father's car,
so at first I didn't see him
sitting behind the wheel
of a shiny blue pickup truck.
"Surprise!" he said to me.
"We traded our car in for this beauty,
right there on the used-car lot."

I got in beside my mother,
who took my brother on her lap,
and when we had to stop
in the heavy downtown traffic,
I felt glad to be sitting so high up.
"It seems safer than a car," said my mother.
"Oh, it *is*," my father said.
Fifteen minutes later, we were out of town,
and he pulled over to the side of the road.
"Who wants to ride in back?" he asked me.
"I do!" I cried.

Riding along under the sky
in the evening air,
as the countryside became more familiar
closer to home,
sitting alone on the floor of the truck,

I started to sing a camp song:
"*Te-ell me wh-hy the stars do shine,*
Te-ell me wh-hy the i-ivy twines . . ."
Then, over the noise of the motor
and the tires on the road,
my mother joined in on a higher note,
harmonizing with me:
"*Te-ell me wh-hy the sky's so <u>blue</u>,*
And I will tell you just why <u>I-I love you</u>."
Without saying anything,
we took deep breaths
and began again together,
this time even sweeter than before:
"*Be-cause God ma-ade the stars to shine,*
Be-cause God ma-ade the i-ivy twine,
Be-cause God ma-ade the sky so <u>blue</u> . . ."

We rode into our driveway,
my father stopped the truck,
and in the silence we finished:
"*Be-cause God made you, that's why I-I love you.*"
The grass, the trees, and our house
all looked gray in the dark,
and I saw my little brother sleeping
when my parents opened their doors
and the ceiling light came on.

A Surprise for My Father

One day, my mother and father
drove into town with my little brother.
I decided to stay at home
and practice the harmonica:
"Wheee-whooo, wheee-whoo, heee-hoo, hee."
From my seat on the porch
I noticed a car
drive by on the highway,
and after a while it came back the other way,
slowed down, turned into our driveway,
and a tall, handsome man got out.
I could see he was a pilot with a broken wing
—I mean, arm.

"Does the doctor live here?" he asked me.
When I said yes, he nodded to the driver,
who waved at him and rode away.
"Please come in," I said.
"My father will be back soon."
"Oh, I hope so," he groaned.
Then he lowered himself into the swing
and shut his eyes,
and I could see that he was in pain.
As soon as he opened them again,
he noticed my harmonica
on the window sill.
"Do you know 'The Handsome Young Airman'?"
he asked me.
"Well, you're—" I began bashfully.

But he had raised his chin,
fixed his eyes on the rafters,
and in a pleasant voice started to sing:
"*A handsome young airman lay dying,*
And as on the airdrome he lay,
To mechanics who 'round him came sighing,
These last parting words he did say:
'Take the cylinders out of my kidneys,
The connecting rods out of my brain,
The crankshaft out of my backbone,
And assemble the engine again.'"
"Oh!" I said, when he was done.
"My father would really love that song.
He was a doctor in the Air Force
when I was born."

The pilot threw his good arm across his eyes
and astonished me by saying:
"You *look* like your father! Sawbones Frankel!
We were in the service together."
"You were?" I exclaimed.
"Sure. I'm still flying—I'm a crop duster.
Gosh, it'll be good to see him again."

My Birthday

On the morning of my birthday,
my parents and little brother kissed me.
They sang "Happy Birthday,"
and when I picked up my napkin,
I found money.
They cried, "That's for a present
from town this afternoon!"
My mother helped me clean my room,
then I held my purse in my lap
on the ride into town.

"Aren't you coming?" I asked my father
when he finally stopped the car.
But he told me to have a good time,
and he'd meet me there at three.
"If I get paints, I'll be an artist,
if I get a book, I'll be an author,
if I get clothes,
I'll be a dress designer," I said,
taking long steps down the street.
I stopped in front of the drugstore.
They had cameras in the window!
I made up my mind and went inside.
I came out into the sunlight
carrying a square black camera
by its neat little handle,

and I had the instruction folder
and an extra roll of film in my purse.
I walked along like a photographer,
staring hard at everything,
wondering if I should take a picture.
When I felt hungry,
I went into the dime store
and sat down at the lunch counter.
I ate my chiliburger slowly,
thinking about the pictures I would take:
the popcorn wagon
that parked near my school sometimes,
and the sun inside our kitchen,
every summer afternoon,
lighting up the sink.

After I paid, I went to the park
and practiced looking at trees
through the viewer.
"So that's what you see," I said to my camera,
because we were partners.
I took a picture of the library
and heard my camera's nice, loud click.
On the way to meet my father,
I vowed to take it everywhere.
"It will be my constant companion," I told him.

Yom Kippur

On the Jewish High Holy Day,
Yom Kippur,
neither my little brother nor I
went to school.
We put on our best clothes
early in the morning,
and I whispered to my brother:
"Be careful when you brush your teeth
not to swallow any water!"
But my mother told me,
"Children don't have to fast all day,"
and she gave us milk and cereal.

Our temple was sixty miles away.
My father drove us there in time
to hear the organ play,
before the rabbi rose and said:
"This is the day of God."
We read the prayer "Aveenu Malkaynu":
"Our Father, our King, we have sinned before Thee.
Our Father, our King, inscribe us for blessing
in the book of life.
Our Father, our King, grant us a year of happiness . . ."
When the morning service was over,
our family walked in the park
and picked up colored autumn leaves.
"I'm hungry," said my brother.

In temple again, we stood and exclaimed:
"Let us adore the ever living God,
and render praise unto Him
who spread out the heavens
and established the earth . . ."
During the rest of the afternoon service,
I looked at the leaves in my prayer book.
My brother slept on my father's arm,
and every time we had to stand,
my father gently moved him over.
Suddenly the shofar blew:
"*Te-keeeeeee-ah!*"
"Good Yontif!" cried my mother.
Everyone shook hands with the rabbi,
and it was dark when we went out,
into the cold air.

We ate at a drive-in on the highway.
My mother said, "We should have a feast,
after praying and fasting all day."
"This seems like one," joked my father.
But after we got home that night,
we sat at the clean kitchen table together
and had apple slices dipped in honey,
"for a sweet year."

Our Friend, Mr. Johnson

From the earliest time I can remember,
my father kept on his desk top
two round seashells called Cowries.
The brown-spotted Tiger Cowrie
had a thin yellow stripe down its back,
and the Golden Cowrie's back
was a deep, shining orange.
First I, and then my brother,
when he got older,
could carefully play with them
on the floor in front of the oil burner.

This is how we played:
One day the two Cowries went for a walk.
Suddenly the Tiger Cowrie turned on his side
and showed his teeth to his friend.
The Golden Cowrie turned on *his* side
and showed *his* teeth!
Then they continued their walk
all around the oil burner,
one in each hand of my little brother.

Sometimes in the evening after supper
my father picked up his guitar
and began strumming.
Then our neighbor, Mr. Johnson,
an old black man
who had arthritis in his hands,
would always hear him and come over.

He couldn't play any more,
but he taught my father some new songs,
like "Crash on the Highway"
and "The Great Speckled Bird,"
and said that he was getting good.
One night while we were all singing
and Mr. Johnson was stamping his feet,
my brother got so carried away
he started to hit the Cowries together.
"Stop!" cried my father. "They'll chip!"
I hurried to the kitchen,
where my mother was working,
and brought back a pot and its lid.
"Now you have a drum," I told him,
but the noise he made with them was deafening,
and our friend, Mr. Johnson, went home.

The next day he returned,
bringing a real African drum.
It had a sweet, small, wild sound,
and my brother played it very rhythmically.
"Thank Mr. Johnson," my father told him.
Tip! Tip! Tap! Tap!
"You're very welcome," said Mr. Johnson.

New Year's Eve

My mother went to the beauty shop
on the morning of New Year's Eve,
and when she came home,
not only was her hair curled,
but the top wave was sprayed gold,
and the rest sparkled
with silver sprinkles!
All day it looked strange
with her house dress and apron.
But after my father came home
and we had dinner,
my little brother and I helped her
do the dishes.

Then she went upstairs
to put on her green taffeta dress,
matching shoes, and pearl jewelry,
so everything was beautiful together.
"How do I look?" asked my father,
to tease her.
"Wonderful!" we shouted.
"Here are some snacks for you,
and this is the telephone number.
Take good care of each other,"
my mother said to us before they left.
First we shared a can of Vienna sausages,
then we listened to the radio.
Next we played some card games.

"Will you tell me a story?"
my brother asked me.
I sat down on the couch beside him
and, in my scariest voice, said:
"It was a *cold* wintry night.
Three thieves sat around the fire.
'Pete,' said the Chief, 'tell us a story.'
'Oak,' said Pete, and the story began:
It was a *cold* wintry night.
Three thieves sat around the fire.
'Pete,' said the Chief, 'tell us a story.'
'Oak,' said Pete, and the story began:
It was a *cold* wintry night."
(My brother started laughing.)

"Three thieves sat around the fire.
'Pete,' said the Chief—"
Just then we heard the front door open
and felt a cold, perfumed wind
as our parents came in!
"Good, you're up!" cried my mother gaily.
"Dad and I left the party early
so we could be with our sweethearts
to welcome in the New Year."

Alberto Giacometti

Sitting on our porch,
I read from a magazine
how inside Paris,
a gay and dreamy city,
there lived a man
named Giacometti.
His hair looked gray
and his clothes and hands were gray
from working in a studio
where even the daylight
streamed in gray.

Its walls were gray,
his pencils, brushes, benches,
bottles, tools, were gray,
and everyone who went to see him
came out covered with the dust
of clay and plaster,
because he was a sculptor.
Giacometti worked hard,
slapping heavy handfuls of wet clay
onto an armature.
Then, dancing around it
like a fighter,
gouging it and scraping it
to make a figure,
he took so much away
it seemed to cry:
"What is man but dust?"

And gasping with despair,
Giacometti swore
that he couldn't create
a single thing he saw.
He also was a painter,
digging long, narrow brushes
into colors of clay.
His canvas on an easel,
he painted in with white and black
and painted out with gray.
He painted in with white and black
and painted out with gray.
Nobody asked him to do it,
and only he cared if he stopped.
He was an artist.

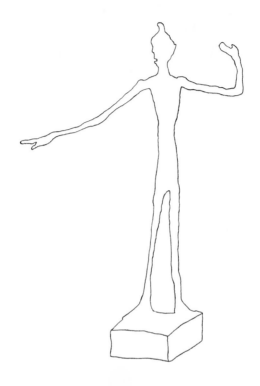

"What is man but dust?"
Giacometti seemed to ask,
as a tall, thin plaster figure
was borne out of his gray studio
for casting into bronze.
And the answer came back:
"Glory!"